MR. GRIGGS' WORK

By Cynthia Rylant   *Illustrated by* Julie Downing

ORCHARD BOOKS · NEW YORK

Text copyright © 1989 by Cynthia Rylant
Illustrations copyright © 1989 by Julie Downing
First Orchard Paperbacks edition 1993

Orchard Books, 95 Madison Avenue, New York, NY 10016

Manufactured in the United States of America. Book design by Mina Greenstein.
The text of this book is set in 17 pt. Hampshire Old Style.
The illustrations are pastel drawings reproduced in full color.

Paperback 10 9 8 7 6 5 4 3

Library of Congress Cataloging-in-Publication Data
Rylant, Cynthia. Mr. Griggs' work / Cynthia Rylant ; illustrations by Julie Downing. p. cm.
"A Richard Jackson book."
Summary: Mr. Griggs so loves his work at the post office that he thinks of it all the time and everything reminds
him of it.
ISBN 0-531-07037-9 (pbk.)
[1. Postal service—Fiction. 2. Occupations—Fiction.] I. Downing, Julie, ill. II. Title. III. Title: Mister
Griggs' work. PZ7.R982Mr 1989 [E]--dc19 88-1484

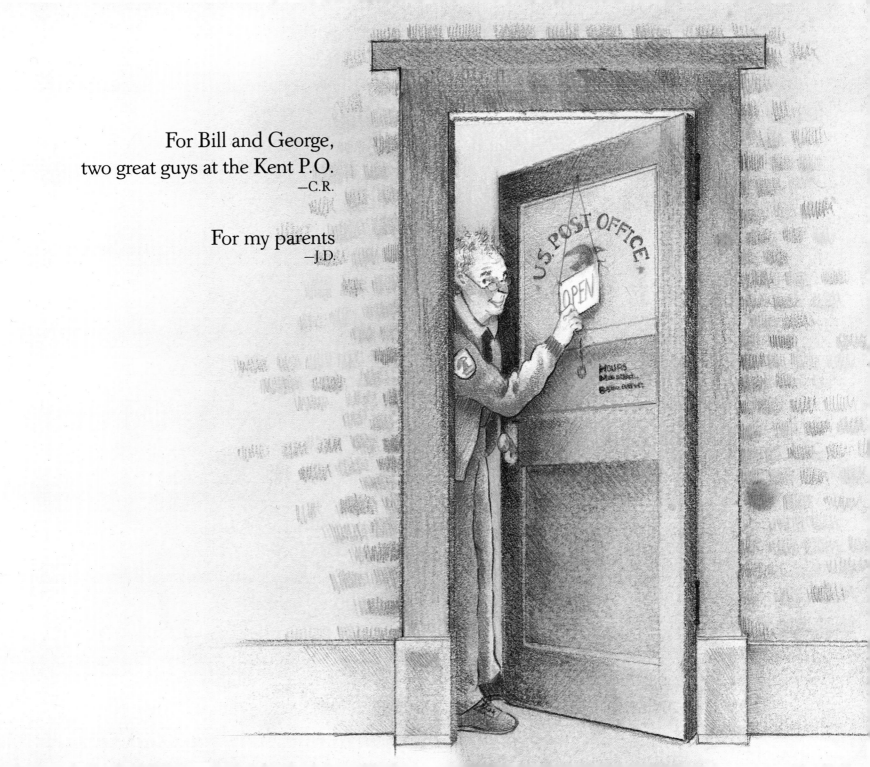

For Bill and George,
two great guys at the Kent P.O.
—C.R.

For my parents
—J.D.

Mr. Griggs worked at the old post office.

He was pretty old himself.

He had spent millions of minutes of his long life shuffling through letters, watching the pictures on the stamps change, punching his First Class puncher, weighing fat brown boxes, and listening to long tales about "The Letter That Never Got There."

Mr. Griggs loved his job.

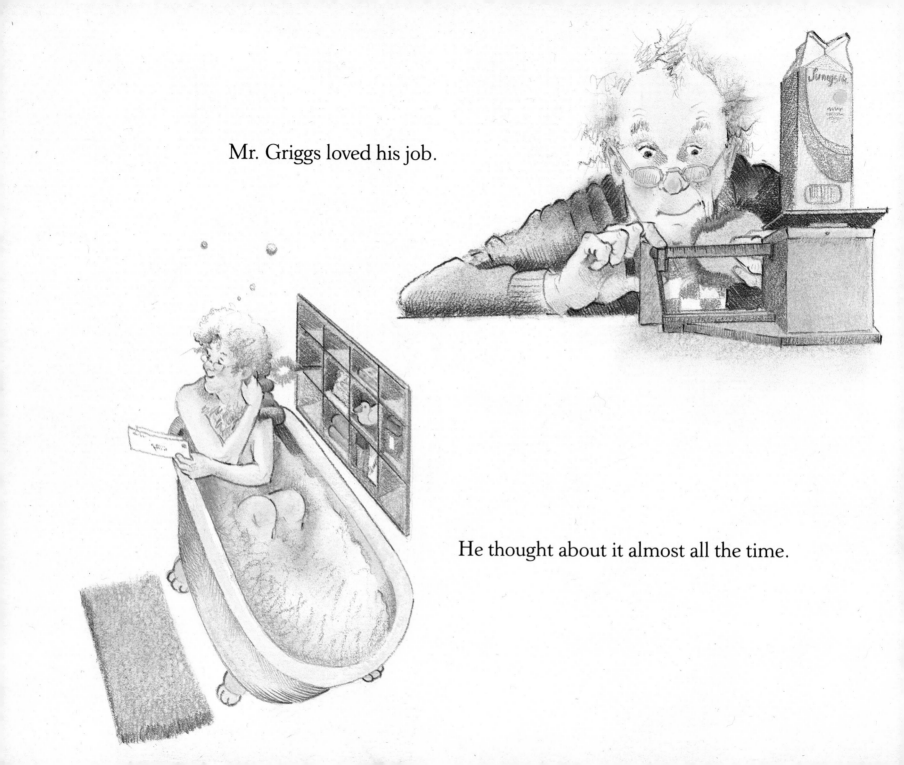

He thought about it almost all the time.

Now and then Mr. Griggs would be washing up his supper dishes when he'd start thinking about the fruitcake Mrs. McTacket had sent her sister fifteen Christmases ago.

That fruitcake had never arrived, and in the middle of his dishes Mr. Griggs would wonder, *Where is that fruitcake?*

Some nights he'd lie in bed wondering how much it would cost to mail a one-pound package to New Zealand or a three-ounce letter to Taiwan.

It was hard not to get up in the middle of the night and go find out. And at times, he just couldn't help himself.

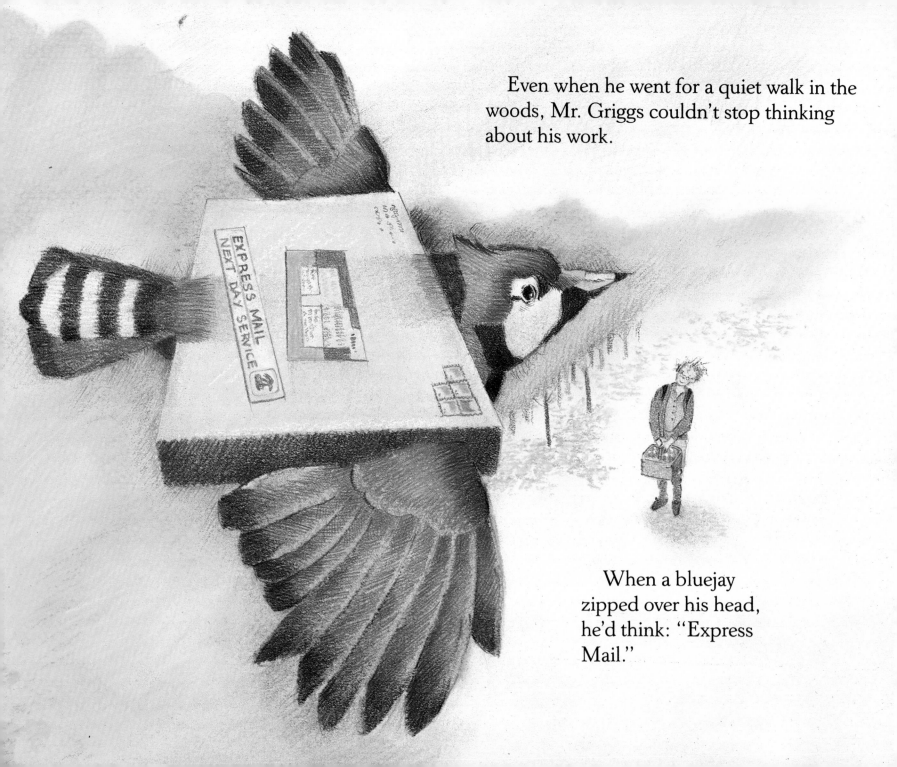

Even when he went for a quiet walk in the woods, Mr. Griggs couldn't stop thinking about his work.

When a bluejay zipped over his head, he'd think: "Express Mail."

When a squirrel darted up a
tree with an acorn in its mouth,
he'd think: "Special Delivery."

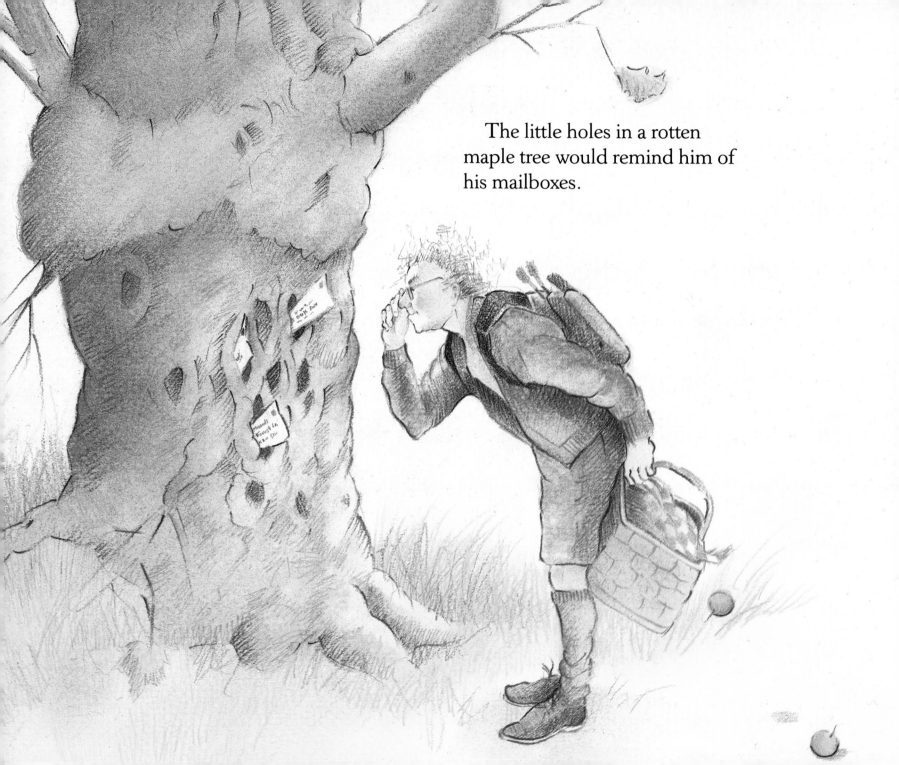

The little holes in a rotten
maple tree would remind him of
his mailboxes.

He couldn't even look at a chipmunk without remembering the chipmunk stamp of 1978. But Mr. Griggs didn't mind. He loved his work.

One day Mr. Griggs became sick. His head ached and his stomach hurt and he lay in bed all day long. It was the first time he'd ever been too sick to go to work, and now someone else was taking care of his post office. Someone else was sorting through Mr. Griggs' letters, someone else was putting pennies and nickels in Mr. Griggs' drawer, someone else was taping up the corners of one of Mr. Griggs' ragged parcels.

Someone else was doing Mr. Griggs' work.

Poor old Mr. Griggs felt like a dead letter.

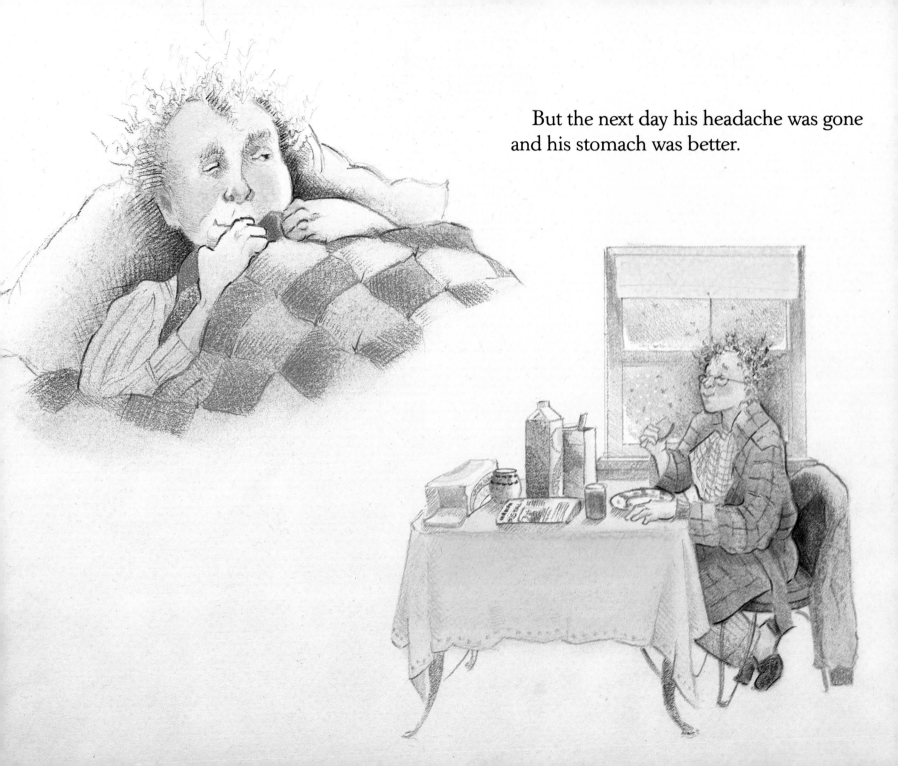

But the next day his headache was gone
and his stomach was better.

He was still tired, though, and because he was moving slower than usual he was a little late leaving for work.

When he finally showed up at the old building, in front of it stood Mrs. Emma Bradshaw (Box 98), Mr. Frank Shrewsberry and his son Junior (Box 171), Miss Sue Ann Huckabee (Box 10), and young Bobby Bricker (Box 21).

Mr. Griggs was so
glad to be back that
he shook hands with
them all and nearly
squeezed the dickens
out of young Bobby.

Then he unlocked the door of his beloved post office. He settled himself behind his little window and to Miss Huckabee, who was first in line, he said, almost gleefully, "First Class or Parcel Post?"

He ran his fingers over his old letter scale, he sniffed at his stamp drawer, he lined up his meters and punchers, and he glanced lovingly at all the brass mailboxes lining the walls.

In all the world that day there was nothing
finer than Mr. Griggs' work.